Appointments with the Little King

by J. Janda

illustrated by William Hart McNichols

Paulist Press

other works by j. janda

Nobody Stop By To See
Hanbelachia
Julian
The Legend of the Holy Child of Atocha
The Legend of St. Christopher

The author wishes to thank William Hart McNichols for his encouragement to retell the legend for a younger audience and Ludvig Nemec for his work, *The Infant of Prague*.

Little King, wherever you are, I hope you are happy with it—and Sister Teresa, I know this little book will find you.

Text design by Ellen Whitney

Janda, J. (James), 1936–
    Appointments with the Little King.

    Summary: On assignment to photograph the Infant Jesus of Prague statue, Mr. Zvonec learns of the legend surrounding the statue's creation and transportation from Spain to Prague.
    1. Infant Jesus of Prague (Sculpture)—Juvenile fiction. 2. Jesus Christ—Art—Juvenile fiction. [1. Infant Jesus of Prague (Sculpture)—Fiction. 2. Jesus Christ—Art—Fiction. 3. Christian life—Fiction] I. McNichols, William Hart, ill. II. Title.
PZ7.J18Ap 1987   [Fic]   87-7324
ISBN 0-8091-2932-9 (pbk.)

Published by Paulist Press
997 Macarthur Boulevard
Mahwah, NJ 07430

Printed and bound in the United States of America

To the Memory of John XXIII

Where there is no love, put love,
And there you will find love.
John of the Cross

foreword

I was taking pictures of the old onion dome churches in Kiev when the meltdown at Chernobyl occurred, and it was in Kiev that I saw him again. This time he was dressed as a little soldier in heavy wool khakis and wearing a little military cap with a red star. Yes, it was the Little King. My first impulse was to run over to speak to him, but he put his finger to his lips, and I understood that, for political reasons, it was at present unwise to approach him. Within a few minutes, though, he was at my side.

"What are you doing here?" I asked.

"And what are you doing here?" he answered. He was smiling. "I am here to command you to write our book."

"Our book?" I asked.

"Yes," he said. "It is time!"

"Not from the beginning."

"Yes, from the beginning, and you must call it, *Appointments with the Little King,* and you must write it for children."

I knew in my heart that it was useless to argue with him; after all, he was the Little King, and I had definitely been part of his little kingdom for some time. So I said, "If you wish, Your Majesty," gave him a chocolate bar, bowed, and turned to leave.

"That was not necessary," he said and laughed.

Other people were laughing too, for after I had bowed to him, I accidentally tripped and bumped into one of the armed guards. I knew it was my time to disappear, though I believe the Little King might still be traveling there.

Yes, I obeyed his command, returned to New York, wrote "our book," asked my friend to illustrate it (he is also a member of the little kingdom), sent it off to a publisher who agreed to publish it, and so here it is—*Appointments with the Little King.*

the assignment in prague

It all began in Prague five years ago when an assignment took me there to the Church of Our Lady of Victory in *Mala Strana,* or Lesser Town, to photograph a famous statue, the statue of the Infant of Prague. A New York firm was doing a book on baroque art (a student text, to be exact) and wanted me to take some photos of this image and other examples of baroque art there.

I had just arrived in Prague, and on the recommendation of a friend, I decided to register at the Inn of the Three Ostriches in *Stare Mesto,* or Old Town, as they call it.

The next morning was bright and sunny, and after a hearty breakfast of goulash and beer, I walked across the old Charles Bridge with its weather-worn saints, over the Vlatava River, to the church.

I arrived shortly after the priest had finished the Mass. A few old people were leaving as I slowly walked up the side aisle to the magnificent shrine of the Infant of Prague. A nun was changing the flowers on the altar.

Ah, but it was beautiful. There was the famous image of the Infant, the little Christ Child, dressed as a king in a red velvet robe and a cape heavily embroidered with gold thread. Over his head was a crown of gold and silver and studded with gems. Little silver cherubs were all around him, and gold rays were behind him, and there was a big silver shell behind his head. There were rings and gold chains on the Infant, and at his feet an ornament of garnets and little diamonds spelled out *Jezis,* the word for Jesus in Czech.

There was a heavy smell of incense in the air, and I was feeling a little light-headed as I set up my tripod and prepared to take several shots. I wanted to take photos from different angles to capture the beauty of this surprising work of art.

I remember that I was looking through the lens of my camera and feeling very happy with what I saw in the frame. I snapped several pictures; it was just the angle I wanted. It seemed to capture the Infant of Prague in all his glory and majesty: I caught the expression on his face, the crown, the right hand raised in blessing, and the left hand holding the orb, the symbol of the world.

Then it happened. The image smiled and pitched his little world to me. "No," I shouted, raised my head, tripped over the tripod, and blacked out.

Later, I remember hearing a gentle voice, and seeing the face of a nun, and realizing I was lying on the cold church floor.

sister teresa

"I am Sister Teresa," she said. "Just relax a few moments. No, please don't try to get up just yet. You passed out for a few seconds."

"My camera, where is it?" I asked.

"Here it is," she said. "Please don't worry. I caught it as you fell. Nothing is damaged." She was speaking with a distinctly British accent.

"Are you from England?" I asked.

"Yes," she said. "I have been doing research on the Little King of Prague. I have been reading all about the Little King and the legends and history connected with him."

"The Little King?" I asked.

"Yes," she said, "that's what I call him. Do you think you can stand up now?"

She helped me up, and though I felt a little weak, I had no trouble moving about.

"Please," she said, "come to our convent. I think it would be good for you to have some tea. One always needs tea after an appointment with the Little King."

"I would love some tea," I said. I was wondering what her words "an appointment with the Little King" had to do with my passing out. (Later I would understand, but I am getting ahead of myself.) "Please lead the way," I said. I picked up the tripod and camera, put them in their cases, and followed Sister Teresa out of the church to the convent where she was staying.

at the convent

From the window of the convent I saw an old woman feeding pigeons: one was perched on her arm and another was just about to land on her head.

I had just finished my first cup of tea when Sister Teresa had stepped out of the room, only to return with a platter of kolaches fresh from the oven. "Here," she said, "you must try some of these."

I didn't protest. Sister Teresa sat down again and joined me.

"Sister," I said, "tell me about this Little King. Who carved the statue? When was it made? Where was it made? How did it get here?"

She paused a few seconds before answering me.

"The image of the Little King, or the Infant of Prague, was brought from Spain to Prague in 1556 by Maria Manriquez de Lara on the eve of her wedding to Lord Vratislav of Pernstyn. Maria and Lord Vratislav lived many happy years together: eventually their family numbered twenty children—"

"Twenty children!" I cut in.

"Twenty children," she repeated, "though not all of them lived. Maria gave the image of the Little King to one of her daughters, Polyxena, who then gave it to the Carmelite monks in Prague in the year 1628."

"But who made the image of the Little King?" I asked, then added, "and who gave it to Maria?"

"It is a beautiful legend," she said.

"Sister, please tell me the legend. I am fascinated with this Little King—as you call him."

"Then I shall tell you the legend," she said.

She paused to sip some tea, and then began the legend.

sister teresa
begins the legend

The candles were burning low on the long oak table covered with wedding presents before the last of the guests left. It was the last night Maria could spend at home with her mother: in the morning, she would be making the long journey from Cordoba in Spain, to Prague in Bohemia—to marry Lord Vratislav.

"Oh Mother," she said, "I am going to miss you." She sat next to her mother on the bench beside the fireplace with its glowing orange embers and began to cry.

Her mother held her until she stopped crying, and then said, "I will miss you too. But, Maria, follow me. I have something very special to give to you. Come."

She took Maria by the hand and led her across the large empty room. Then she lifted the tapestry on the wall and pushed the edge of a wood panel. Suddenly, a little door sprang open, and there in the hidden niche stood the image of the Little King wearing a white gown.

"Is he for me?" Maria asked.

"Yes," said her mother. "He is your wedding present, your Little King. You must take him to Prague with you. He will help you remember me—and to pray to the Child Jesus who listens to all our needs."

Then her mother took the image out of the niche and placed it in Maria's arms.

"He is so beautiful," said Maria.

"Look," said her mother, "with his right hand he is blessing us, and with his left hand he is holding the world. This means that the Little King has nothing but love in his heart for us, and that we should never worry or be sad, because he holds the world in his hand and carries it very carefully."

"Yes, I see," said Maria.

"He is your *piccolo rex*, your *Gesu Bambino*," she said in her native Italian. (*Piccolo rex* means "little king." Can you guess what *Gesu Bambino* means?)

"Oh how can I thank you, mother!" she said as she car-

ried the little image back to the bench where she sat down and waited for her mother to join her. And once her mother was seated next to her, she asked, "But where did you find this beautiful little image?"

Her mother leaned back against the bench and spoke slowly—at first. "Maria, I don't know how to tell you this. Even now, I can hardly believe how I found him."

"You must tell me," Maria said. "I must know all about him."

And then her mother, Doña Isabella de Bresagno, began her story.

doña isabella begins her story

Some years ago, when you were in Prague, Doña Dolorado de Vives sent me a letter saying that her husband had just died, and that she would very much like me to pay her a visit in Nueva Caseta. Her letter took me by surprise, but since you were away, and I was feeling lonely, I decided to visit her.

And it was a most beautiful visit! It was so good to see my old friend again. I found it difficult to say goodbye, and I felt sad as I left her. But since it was late summer, and all the flowers were in full bloom, and all the trees were loaded with leaves and fruit—oranges and lemons—and because of the sweet smell of flowers in the air, I forgot my sadness and began to enjoy the coach ride back.

Well, it was all too beautiful to pass by. I ordered Murgo and Lorenzo to stop the coach so that I could walk off alone and examine this place more closely—to enjoy the lovely trees. They stopped the coach, and I got out and walked off alone through the many trees. I walked and walked through the trees. I was smelling pine in the air and walking on a carpet of their dead red needles. Finally I was ready to return to the coach, when in the distance, through the trees, I suddenly noticed an old ruined building of stone. Out of curiosity, I walked through the trees until I reached it and found that it was overgrown with ivy, and that on the side of the wall closest to me was a door with an old metal knocker turned green.

Something inside me made me knock three times. I didn't know why I did it, but to my complete surprise the top half of the door opened, and a kindly faced monk with a long white beard appeared.

"Doña Isabella de Bresagno," he said, "please come in. I have something to give to you."

How he knew my name I will never know.

Well, he opened the lower part of the door and led me down a long corridor into the chapel, and then into the sacristy, where he opened a cabinet and took out the Little King you are now holding in your arms—and put him in my arms.

I could think of nothing to say, but he said, "Doña Isabella, this little image of the Christ Child is not for you. You must give it to your daughter, Maria Manriquez de Lara, who will marry Lord Vratislav of Pernstyn. She must take this image to the people of Bohemia to give them hope, so that they will be reminded that the Holy Child loves them and is the Prince of Peace. You look hungry," he said. "Come, follow me."

I did as I was told, since I could no longer think. How he knew your name or that you would marry Lord Vratislav—when I didn't even know this at the time—was beyond me.

He led me into an empty dining hall, chose a table nearest the door, and bade me to sit and eat. There was bread and wine on the table.

Well, I could not eat—though I did accept a glass of wine. Strengthened by the wine, I finally said, "Venerable Father, who made this beautiful, beautiful image which you have just given to me?"

"Brother Joseph," he said.

"Perhaps I can meet him," I said, "and tell him how pleased I am with his gift."

"He is dead," the old monk said.

"Dead!" I gasped. "Oh, I am sorry." Then, without my asking him, he began to tell me the story of Brother Joseph.

the old monk begins the story of brother joseph

This is a very old monastery, and two years ago, there were only four of us left—myself, and Brother Joseph, and two other monks whose names are not necessary for you to know. Brother Joseph was the youngest of the four of us; in fact, he was still a novice.

Brother Joseph had one wish: he wanted to see the Christ Child before he died. He was a wood-carver, and I suppose that he wanted to see the Christ Child so that he could carve an accurate image of him. He carved many little statues over the years, but none of them pleased him. As you will see, he was getting in practice for the real thing—the Christ Child did actually appear to him. His wish came true.

There he was one day, scrubbing away on the floor in the kitchen, when suddenly this little boy appears and says, "Brother Joseph, you do know how to scrub floors! Do you know the Hail Mary?"

Well, Brother Joseph says, "Hail, Mary, full of grace, and blessed is the fruit of thy womb, Jesus—"

"That's me," cuts in the Christ Child. "Carve an image of me so people won't forget me, so people won't forget that I love them, so people won't forget that I wish them peace."

"I'll start now," said Brother Joseph and ran to get his wood, hammer, and chisels. When he got back, the Child had just disappeared. Yes, Brother Joseph was a bit disappointed, I confess, but he knew in his heart that he'd see the Child again.

Well, Brother Joseph lost no time. From memory, he started to work on a piece of wood as best he could, and soon it began to look just like the Child he had seen. Then he covered the whole thing with wax, and wouldn't you know—it looked even better.

To make a long story short, the next time the Christ Child appeared (accompanied by little angels, I might add), Brother Joseph was all ready: the image was almost finished and standing in front of him on the workbench when the Christ Child appeared. All he had to do was to put on some finishing touches of paint—which he did do—and when we found him, he was dead.

Doña Isabella de Bresagno gasped again.

"That's just the half of it," the old monk said. "Can you imagine what I felt like when he visited me in a dream—from the dead?"

"Not from the dead!" whispered Doña Isabella.

"From the dead," the old monk said, and went on: "In the dream, Brother Joseph was standing at the foot of my bed and speaking to me as plain as day."

"Venerable Father," he said (that's what they all called me because I was the oldest—though thanks be to God, I survived them all), "Venerable Father, you are not to keep that image here for my brothers, but to give it to Doña Isabella de Bresagno who will visit you here. She must not keep it either, but must give it to her daughter, Maria Manriquez de Lara, who must take it to Prague, where she will marry Lord Vratislav of Pernstyn. It is the wish of the Little King not to be forgotten there. Through this reminder, my little image of wood, the people of Prague, and all over the world, will be reminded to keep peace and to learn of his little kingdom." Then, just like that, he was gone.

"But were you not afraid?" asked Doña Isabella.

"No, why should I be afraid?" he asked. "Brother Joseph would never hurt a fly when he was alive. And besides, when you meditate every day, nothing ever really surprises you, or, I should say, shakes you up."

doña isabella finishes her story

Maria was yawning, and the embers in the fireplace were burning low. Maria pulled her shawl more closely around herself. The night was growing cold.

"I see you are getting sleepy, Maria," her mother said, "so I will finish the story."

"As you know by now, I had very little to do with your wedding gift, but to give it to you, and to tell you the story—yet, even now, I doubt that it happened, even though I see you with the Little King in your arms. Take him to Bohemia, to Prague. We must do his little will."

sister teresa finishes the legend

And now Sister Teresa was finishing the legend, pulling the last threads of the story together.

"Yes, Maria did carry the Little King to Prague. You saw him today, in the Church of Our Lady of Victory. The rest of the story you already know."

"But, Sister," I said, "the rest of the story I do not know. What happened to the Little King after Polyxena gave him to the Carmelite monks? And the Little King is wearing real clothes: a real cape, a royal robe, a real crown. I have never seen a statue wearing real clothes. Where did the clothes come from? And, I'm told, there are images of this Little King all over the world. How did so many people come to know him? And—"

"I don't know your name. What is your name?" was Sister Teresa's answer to my questions.

"My name?" I asked.

"You do have one, do you not?" she said and smiled.

"Yes," I said. "My name is Anton. Anton Zvonec."

"Good, now I know your name," she said. "Mr. Zvonec, you have asked me many questions. I believe you know many of the answers in your heart. At present, I have some tasks to do. Can you call tomorrow? I am free from seven until eight in the morning. Tomorrow, I will be happy to attempt to answer some of your questions."

"Seven? In the morning?" I asked.

"Correct," she said, "seven in the morning."

Now I could think of nothing to say. "Seven in the morning," I thought. "What time will I have to get up to be here at seven?"

Finally I got up, picked up my equipment, walked to the door, turned and said, "Sister Teresa, I thank you. Tomorrow, at seven in the morning."

"I didn't finish the story," she said. "Doña Isabella de Bresagno went back several times to the exact same spot, but she never found the monastery—and for that matter, she never saw the old monk again."

"Oh no," I said.

"Oh, yes," she said.

the appointment with sister teresa

The next morning I was up at five. To my surprise, I was wide awake. I was excited about seeing Sister Teresa again, and Prague fascinated me too. I couldn't see enough of it. I loved to walk the streets and see all the medieval buildings and houses.

And the mysterious legend Sister Teresa had told me took me back to my childhood and all the stories of castles and kings and enchanted forests. Yes, the unexpected meeting with Sister Teresa and the stories she told me made me feel like a child again, excited about everything.

Soon I was again walking across the old Charles Bridge over the Vlatava River flowing so silently on and on at six in the morning. I passed old trees just starting to bud with leaves. I saw pigeons pecking on the pavements for crumbs, and people walking to work. It was as if I was seeing for the first time, like a blind man who had just received his sight, in the early morning light. The sky at this hour was the color of a pink rose.

As I approached the convent I looked at my watch and realized that I was a half an hour early. It was six-thirty, to be exact. And as I approached the stoop, I saw that Sister Teresa was just opening the door. Sparrows were chattering and flying up to the eaves carrying bits of paper and string in their beaks to build nests. Spring had come to Prague.

"Good morning, Mr. Zvonec," Sister Teresa said.

"Good morning," I replied.

I could smell coffee brewing and fresh baked bread.

She again led me into the parlor with its big window looking out onto the street. The table was spread with a plate, knife, fork, and spoon, a bowl of butter, a dish of plum jam, coffee cups and saucers, and a cutting board with its knife and a fresh loaf of braided bread sprinkled with poppy seeds.

"Sit down and eat, Mr. Zvonec," she said as she poured me a steaming cup of coffee. "Enjoy your breakfast. I will return shortly." Then she left.

She didn't have to say this a second time. The walk to the convent had given me quite an appetite. No, I did not go hungry.

When I had finished, I leaned back, lit a cigarette, and felt peaceful and happy inside. I was enjoying the morning silence.

my questions are answered

Sister Teresa returned, cleared the table, poured me more coffee, and then sat down.

"Why do people give gifts?" she suddenly asked.

"Why do people give gifts?" I repeated, surprised with her question. "Well," I began, "to show other persons that they love them, or appreciate them, or to thank them for something."

"That is correct," she said. "Now you know why the Little King has all those robes, rings, capes, and even a little crown. They were all gifts, each one of them—from people who wanted to thank him for a gift he had given to each of them. It was a way of saying, 'Thank you.'"

"This I know, but who first dressed the Little King?" I persisted.

"I knew you would ask that," Sister Teresa said, and then she began to tell me the story about who had made the Little King his first suit of clothes.

the little king's first suit of clothes

Of all of Maria's many children, Polyxena, from the time she was a very little girl, took a very special interest in the Little King. Her mother would often find her talking to the Little King and holding him as if he were her own doll.

One day, while Polyxena was holding him in her lap, she asked, "Mother, where did the Little King come from?"

"Come, sit next to me, and I will tell you the story of where the Little King came from." And then Maria told her little daughter the wonderful story of the wedding present which I have told you.

After Maria had finished the story, Polyxena suddenly said, "He must be cold. All he is wearing is a nightshirt."

This took her mother by surprise, but she said, "Well, that is true. I never thought of that. What do you think we should do?"

Then Polyxena said, "I think we should make him some clothes."

"That is a wonderful idea," said her mother. "I know how to sew. Will you help me make him some clothes? They must be very special, for he is a king."

And so Maria took Polyxena by the hand to the old trunk where she stored the clothes she wore before she was married. She opened it and showed her little daughter many of her old clothes. There was a blue silk dress, a green satin dress, and a dress made of yellow and white brocade.

"I think we should use this one," said Polyxena as she pulled out a red velvet gown. "It has gold trimmings. This will look best on the Little King."

Then Maria drew a pattern on paper and showed Polyxena how to pin the pattern to the cloth and how to cut around it. When Polyxena had finished, her mother stitched the red velvet together and added some gold lace for trimming, and finally she let Polyxena dress the Little King for the first time.

And that is how the Little King got his first suit of clothes.

sister teresa tells more about
the little king

"And that is the beginning of the custom of dressing the Little King. Later it became a way of thanking the Little King for a favor received. You see," she continued, "whenever people ask the Little King for something, he always answers them. That is why he has so many suits of clothes."

"Always?" I asked.

"Always," she answered.

"Then I would like to meet this Little King in person," I said, "and find out all about him and his little kingdom."

"You will," she answered.

Her quick answer took me by surprise. I could think of nothing to say.

"It all began with Father Cyril," she said.

"Father Cyril?" I asked.

"Yes," she said. "Because of him, we have the image of the Little King. The other monks would have thrown the damaged figure out, were it not for Father Cyril."

"Damaged? How was the Little King damaged?"

"Around that time, soldiers were occupying Prague," she began. "The monks had fled. The soldiers forced their way into the monastery and destroyed much of it—including the chapel. They even cut a hand off the image of the Little King, and then threw him on a trash heap. When they finally left, the monks decided to return to their monastery. Father Cyril was one of them. The first thing he did was to look for the image, because it meant very much to him. The Little King had given Father Cyril a very special gift—and he never forgot about this."

"What was this special gift the Little King gave to Father Cyril?" I asked.

Then Sister Teresa began the story of Father Cyril's gift from the Little King.

sister teresa tells the story of father cyril

Shortly after Polyxena had given the image of the Little King to the Carmelite monks in Prague, Father Cyril came there from Germany. He wanted to be a monk, and he was sent to the monastery in Prague to live with the monks to see if this was the life for him.

It was not easy for him. He was very lonely, because he missed his family and friends. Then, too, everybody in Prague was living in fear; soldiers were nearing the city and many of the people were leaving for safety. And so, because of this fear of war and his own loneliness, he grew very sad and miserable. In fact, by Christmas Eve, he felt so terrible that he couldn't sleep. In desperation, he went to the chapel and prayed before the image of the Little King. His only prayer was, "Oh Little King, help me. I am so miserable, I want to die."

The Little King heard his prayer. Suddenly he was no longer lonely. He was no longer afraid. He was happy again. His heart was filled with peace.

As the Carmelite records show, he himself told his story to the other monks, and then to everyone else who would listen, because the Little King had listened to his sad prayer and made him happy again.

i ask more questions

"Now," said Sister Teresa, "have I answered all of your questions?"

"Not all," I said, "but I suppose it was Father Cyril who looked for the Little King and found him on the trash heap."

"That is correct," Sister Teresa said. "And it was Father Cyril who had the hand replaced. He even convinced the other monks to place the image of the Little King in the church so others could meet him, rather than keep him in their own chapel. He knew in his heart how people need images of hope—reminders. Yes, we have Father Cyril to thank for the image of the Little King today."

She was looking out the window. I looked too. An old man was helping a blind boy cross the street.

"Mr. Zvonec," she began, "I believe God wants to be known as a little child. A child rules not with fear and terror, but with love and need. The world must know that the Little King does not come to us with swords and guns, but with a plea—for us to become his parent, his friend, to help him rule with gentleness, forgiveness, and love. No, in the little kingdom, there is no room for fear—only meekness, trust, and telling the truth."

I looked at my watch. It was eight o'clock, the time for me to leave.

"Sister," I said a bit nervously, "as I was taking those pictures of the Little King yesterday—before I blacked out—it seemed as though the Little King threw his world to me. He must have trusted me to catch it, not to drop it. That is when I blacked out. What could that mean?"

"Well, I think, among other things, that the Little King wants to play with you. Why else would a child throw his ball to you?" she asked. "I am happy you told me this. I feel you will have many appointments with the Little King."

I passed over her answer, and asked another question. "I know it is time for me to go, but—"

"But why are there images of the Little King all over the world?" she asked, reading my mind. "You will have that answer once you become friends with him, Mr. Zvonec."

"This I believe," I said, "but I want to know what the Little King means to you?"

She paused for a second or two, then very seriously said, "This lovely city of Prague, this little country called Czechoslovakia—our world—our planet—has seldom known peace. The history of our world is one of war, of violence, of destruction. People of the big kingdoms believe this is the only way to survive. The Little King will have none of that. His little kingdom is quite different. That is all I will say. He will teach you the rest. Expect a few appointments with the Little King."

I got up, shook hands with Sister Teresa, thanked her for the fine breakfast, and walked to the door she was opening for me. I walked outside, went down the stoop, and turned to wave goodbye.

"Mr. Zvonec," she called.

"Yes?" I said.

"I predict appointments with the Little King."

back to new york

I returned to New York, developed the negatives, and was very pleased with the prints. So too was the New York firm who commissioned me—they paid me royally.

In less than a month, I received another assignment. I had almost forgotten about my "appointments with the Little King" and Sister Teresa when I received a postcard in the mail. On it was a handwritten poem and it was signed by Sister Teresa.

The poem was entitled, "Mi Casa, Su Casa" which is a greeting the Spanish use when welcoming a guest. It means, "My house is your house." I thought you might like to read her poem, so I pass it on to you.

And you will find, if you continue to read, that Sister Teresa's predictions came true—for now I will tell all about my appointments with the Little King.

Mi Casa, Su Casa

The door now stands open.
You need not knock.
Come in, Little King, come in.

There is no fuel,
The hearth is cold,
But you are expected within.

This house now stands empty,
This house is bare,
And you are sorely wanted here.

It needs an owner,
Fuel, fire, and light,
Your presence and your hands.

Yours is the title,
Yours is the right,
As long as it may stand.

Sister Teresa

Mr. Anton Zvonec
361 Gonzaga avenue
Brooklyn,
New York
11215

U.S.A.

rio de janeiro

It was in Rio de Janeiro where I had my first appointment with the Little King. I was taking photos at the famous *Carneval* festival there for a travel magazine in the States.

The festival was at its height. Everywhere there was food and food vendors, and, of course, the smell of sausage frying—and every kind of pastry. And there was music that never seemed to stop. It was in the air: steel drum bands, and bongos—the rhythm of the bongos, as steady as the pulse of the human heart. And everybody was dancing. It was a festival of colors and the most extravagant costumes I had ever seen. And even the children were in on it. It was a photographer's dream.

I had used up several roles of film and decided to rest. I bought a papaya drink and sat on a wooden crate to watch the crowd.

Then it happened. I felt a tug on my shirt sleeve and realized that a child was climbing on my lap.

"And who are you?" I asked, helping him get adjusted.

"I am a king," he said.

"A king," I said. "I am honored."

He was wearing a gold paper crown, and of course he had his rings, gold shoes—oh yes, and a red silk cape trimmed with gold.

"And where is your kingdom?" I asked.

"There," he said and pointed to the people dancing.

"But I don't see your soldiers and guards," I said.

"I have none," he replied.

"You don't?"

"No," he said.

"But every king has armies, and tax collectors, and guards, and—"

"No they don't," he said.

"They don't? Well, then, a castle—you must have a castle?"

"No castle," he said.

"Swords?" I asked.

"No swords."

"Guns?"

"No guns."

"Cannons?"

"No cannons."

"But do your subjects obey you?" I teased him.

"If they are smart they do," he said, then smiled and added, "Sometimes, but not all the time."

I could not get over him!

"And will you visit me again, O Little King?"

"Do you want me to?" he asked.

"Oh yes," I said.

The next second he jumped off my lap and was easily lost in the crowd.

new york

The next time I met the Little King, he was in disguise—he was dressed as a hippie, with beads, a shirt embroidered with flowers and the word "peace," and he had bare feet.

It was a crowded New York street, and at first I did not recognize him, but then he smiled at me and I walked faster to catch up with him.

"Why do you dress like that, Little King?" I asked.

"Why do you dress like that?" he replied with my question.

Of course this took me by surprise. For some reason, I had expected a reasonable answer. I had to think for a moment, then said, "I dress this way because my clothes are comfortable and—"

"So are mine," he cut in, then added, "You may continue."

Well, I was quite taken aback with his quick mind, so I had to repeat myself. "I dress this way because my clothes are comfortable," and added, "and respectable."

"What does respectable mean?" he asked.

"Respectable means—" (I had to have time to think) "Respectable means trying to do what most people do."

"Most Africans, Eskimos, and fishermen would find your clothes quite impractical," he said. "They would never wear them."

"You win," I said.

This time my answer surprised him.

"That is not the point," he said, then turned and fled.

"Come back, Little King," I said. "I will die without you."

I ran after him, but he was lost in the crowd.

I returned to my apartment wondering what I had said to offend him. It was the word "win." I had said, "You win." How could he have taken offense at that? I would have taken that as a compliment.

Later, I realized how insensitive I had been. That was no way to talk to a child. I should have begun by saying, "How good to see you," or "How are you, my friend?" But, then, I really did not know him and would probably never see him again.

south africa

My work with the American embassy as a photographer took me to South Africa where the whites were warring with the blacks and vice versa. Much to my surprise, it was there in the midst of the violence, fear, and misunderstanding that I met the Little King again.

This time he was dressed not as a hippie or a king, but as an Afrikaner or Dutch boy—quite smart, I thought, in his freshly ironed khakis. I ran through the Sunday morning crowd to be with him.

"Little King," I shouted, "how good to see you! How are you, my friend?"

"I need you," he said.

"But how could you need me?" I asked.

"I need you," he repeated. "Please, take me into that church. With you, they will let me in."

"I don't see why they won't let you in—"

"They won't," he cut in.

"Well, if that will make you happy, I will take you in."

"Promise?" he said.

"Yes," I said.

"Then I will meet you there, in front of that church, in half an hour." He turned and disappeared into a side street.

The time passed quickly. It was one of those warm sunny Sunday mornings, and I was enjoying watching all the people going into the church in their Sunday clothes, and of course I was happy to be with the Little King again.

I was just checking my watch and standing in front of the church when I heard his voice again. He could be very punctual.

"Now you may take me in."

I turned and couldn't believe my eyes. There he was, wearing the same clothes, but looking exactly like a black child, except for his blue eyes. He had done an impeccable job with the brown grease paint. His black woolly wig looked exactly as though it grew from his head.

"You little actor," I said. "Come, let's go in."

I took his hand, and we walked up the steps. On passing through the main door, a very tall usher blocked our way and with a kindly voice said, "I'm terribly sorry, sir, but we cannot let blacks in."

"But he is just a child," I said.

"He is a child, but a black child," said the usher, then added again, "We do not allow blacks in."

"But a black child is a child of God," I said.

The usher bristled, but tried to maintain a respectable composure.

"Look," he said. "If you don't leave, I'll personally throw you and your kid out."

"My kid!" I said. "Look here, I am with the United States embassy and this child is really white."

I reached into my pocket for a handkerchief to rub some grease paint off the Little King to prove my point, but when I turned, he was not there. Yes, he had disappeared again.

the airport

My assignment in South Africa was completed, and I was in a bad mood. As I was packing to leave, I felt angry and helpless: I felt angry because, well, the Little King had disappeared on me once again; I felt helpless because I had to see children suffer, and there wasn't a thing I could do about it. The Little King was teaching me some hard lessons.

And who was he? Where did he come from? Where did he live?

A Little King! He had no power. He needed me, and I was of no help. What a joke, a sad joke!

I was at the airport early, and as I had some time to kill, I decided to buy a chocolate bar. I was about to pay the lady at the counter when I heard the familiar voice again.

"Please, will you buy one for me too?"

This time he was wearing a sailor suit.

"I decided to see you off," he said.

I said nothing, paid for two chocolate bars, and gave one to him. He immediately tore off the wrapper, dropped it in the trash can, and bit into the bar.

"Let's sit over there," I said and led him to an empty corner of the waiting room.

We sat down.

"You look angry," he said.

"Me? Why should I be angry?" I said.

"Tell the truth," he said.

"Not that," I said.

"The truth," he said.

"Well," I began (squirming in my chair). "Well, if you really want to know, I really miss you when you are not here, and I get angry with you when I don't see you for a long time, and I have no way of reaching you, or letting you know that I want to see you again, and you keep disappearing on me, and—

"Go on," he said.

"And if you really are my friend, that is no way to treat me. Where can I find you? Where is your little kingdom? Where do you live?"

The Little King pointed to my heart.

"My heart?" I asked.

"Yes," he said. "That is where I live."

"But where is your little kingdom?" I asked.

"Only there," he said.

Yes, I was confused, too confused to say anything more.

"It is time to board your plane," he said. "I will visit you soon again."

"Promise?" I said.

"Yes," he said.

on the plane

During the flight back to New York, I was lost in my own thoughts. I was thinking about the Little King. I would ask him questions in my mind, and answers would come from my heart.

I would think, "Little King, are you there?" and "Of course!" would come the answer. I knew he would never just answer, "Yes."

And then I would think, "Do you really come from God?" and he would answer, "Yes, but so do you."

"That is true," I continued, "but you are very special," and he said, "So are you."

And then I asked, "But why do you need me?" and he answered, "Because I am a child, but so are you."

"Yes, that is quite true," I said, thinking that I've felt like a child most of my life.

"I know you have," he cut in, reading my thoughts. "I am every child—"

"And every child is you," I finished.

Then I began to worry and said, "But when will people realize this—before it is too late?"

And he said, "Now I will tell you some little kingdom secrets. The first is that it is never too late. The second is that people in my little kingdom live all over the world, and that they will always be there when you need them. The third little kingdom secret is—"

"But, Little King," I cut in, "what do we do when people are mean and cruel?"

"You will always know in your heart what to do," he answered. "The third little kingdom secret is this, 'Where there is no love, put love, and there you will find love.'"

back to prague

I was very happy the following summer because a new assignment took me back once again to Prague.

Prague, the home of my grandparents, the city of spires and steeples, the city of saints, the heart of Europe. Tribe upon tribe, kingdom upon kingdom, government upon government—all wanted this city, this land, this people. "Who controls Prague controls Europe," a statesman had said.

Prague, the heart of Europe! Though many invaded you, though many conquered you, though many claimed you—they could not possess you, they could not kill your spirit, they could not stamp out your hope.

And with each conquest, castles arose; and with each invasion, churches arose; and with each violence, monuments arose, symbols of power, symbols of conquest in stone. But your people still speak Czech, still have their customs, their music, their art, their dances.

It was at a country wedding that I saw him again. He looked like a meadow in spring—white, red, blue, yellow, green—in his white linen shirt with flowers embroidered around the collar and cuffs of his sleeves. He wore a black felt hat stuck with a red carnation and a spray of green. He wore a black vest bordered with silver beads, and a black apron fringed with red and heavily embroidered with white daisies and meadow flowers. I felt proud of him. I felt that he was my son.

He was dancing. Everybody was dancing—the young and old, the married and single.

When the musicians paused to announce the next dance, I caught his eye, or maybe he caught mine.

"Dance with us," I understood him to say in Czech, and in spite of my American clothes, he took my hand and led me in. I tried to follow the steps, but he shouted, "Don't worry. Just dance."

And I did. I just danced. I danced with my Little King. I danced all night—sometimes with him, sometimes without him, but I could not worry because I knew he was there.

the last photographs

Before my return to the States, I planned to spend an afternoon with Sister Teresa, but she had returned to England—so I decided to spend the afternoon at the Church of Our Lady of Victory to take some final pictures of the Infant of Prague for my own collection.

As I was looking through the lens of my camera to focus on the Infant, again the image moved, and I heard the voice of my Little King.

"After you take my picture, please help me take off this crown and these heavy robes. I can hardly move in them."

"Be patient," I said and snapped a few more pictures. "Finished," I said.

"When will people learn that in the little kingdom, every person is a king," he said, then added, "and that acts of cruelty are forbidden?"

"Ah, you must be patient," I said. "Human beings learn very slowly." I sat down on the altar step and he joined me. He took off his cape and placed it on my shoulder—the crown he placed on my head.

Again he read my thoughts and said, "Don't worry, nobody will come in. This church mostly attracts tourists—"

"Like me?" I asked.

"Yes," he said and became quite serious.

"Tell me," he said, "What does it mean to you—the little kingdom?"

"Well, my little friend—"

"That is a perfect way to begin," he cut in, then said, "Continue."

"My dearest friend," I continued, "in your kingdom, your little kingdom, everyone is a king and ought to be treated as such." I knew this would please him because that was what he had been trying to teach me.

"Go on," he said.

"Everyone is welcome here. It has no boundaries, no state lines, no maps, no armies, no weapons, no taxes, no tax collectors, no official membership: cruelty must never be chosen."

"You understand," he said. "I have no castle, no armies. I can only live—"

"In people's hearts," I finished.

"Yes, that is true," he said.

I became amazed how sad and solemn he had become.

"You look sad," I said. "You should be happy. My heart is your home."

"But many people won't open the door," he said. "Many will not let me in," and he began to cry.

Yes, he was crying. My Little King was crying. All I could do was put my arms around him and hold him—for I knew that what he said was true.

I did not know what to say, when suddenly I remembered something he had said.

"My dearest friend, where there is no love, put love, and there you will find love."

"Yes, that is true," he said. "We both have much to do."

postscript

On my flight back to New York, I was a little sad, but refreshed and renewed, for I knew that wherever I went, the Little King would be with me. I knew that I would meet him now and then; I was now part of the little kingdom, and definitely I had something to do. We both had something to do.

Yes, the Little King had found a home—the only place he can survive—in a human heart.

The more you will honor me,
The more I will bless you.
The Little King